# ARCHIESAURUS

Written By **Su Pheng Lim**     Illustrated by **Christie Tan**

Text © Su Pheng Lim 2020
Illustrations © Christie Jia-Wen Tan 2020

First Published 2020

ISBN 978-1-5272-6894-4

HARDCOVER AND PAPERBACK EDITION ALSO AVAILABLE.

THIS BOOK BELONGS TO :

# Welcome Kids, Parents, Teachers, and Readers!

### *Phonemes (sounds) focus in this book:*
- Fundamental sounds (Recommended for ages 3-5): s, a, t, p
- Advanced sounds (Recommended for ages 4-8 including graphemes): "or", "ch", "ee"
- Graphemes (different ways to spell one sound) included: or (ore, au, our, aw), ch (tch, ture), e (ie, ee, ea, y, ey)

### *For Parents/Teachers before reading:*
Front cover (Check my child/student's prediction skills)

### *Prompting questions:*
- Who can you see in the front cover?
- What do you think is going to happen in the story?
- Where do you think the story is going to be set?

### *Recommended for all ages*
Emotional Intelligence Questions:

- Discuss what it means to be "resilient". (Being resilient means that when we make mistakes, we have courage to learn from them and then move to bigger and better things.)
- Do you think that you are resilient? Why? Why not? Give some examples.
- When was the last time that you felt like something was too hard?
- How did you react or feel? What did you learn about yourself?

Now, enjoy going on an adventure with Archie and Ruby that is filled with fun, excitement, and resilience building challenges!

Note: Not all graphemes and represented phonemes are listed and this is a guide only.

# ARCHIESAURUS

Written By **Su Pheng Lim**     Illustrated by **Christie Tan**

Archie put on his dinosaur costume
and **roared mightily** into the mirror.

He **curled** his fingers like **claws** in the air.

Then, he **jumped** and **stomped** to show **his great** dinosaur strength.

Suddenly, as he looked out the window, he couldn't **believe** his eyes!

"Mum! Dad! Look!", Archie called, "Ruby is in the backyard!"

4

**THUMP...**

**THUMP...**

**THUMP...**

Ruby's **stompy** feet accidentally **stepped** on Mum's flower bed.

**SWISH!**

**BAM!**

She **slipped** and **bumped** her head on the old treehouse.

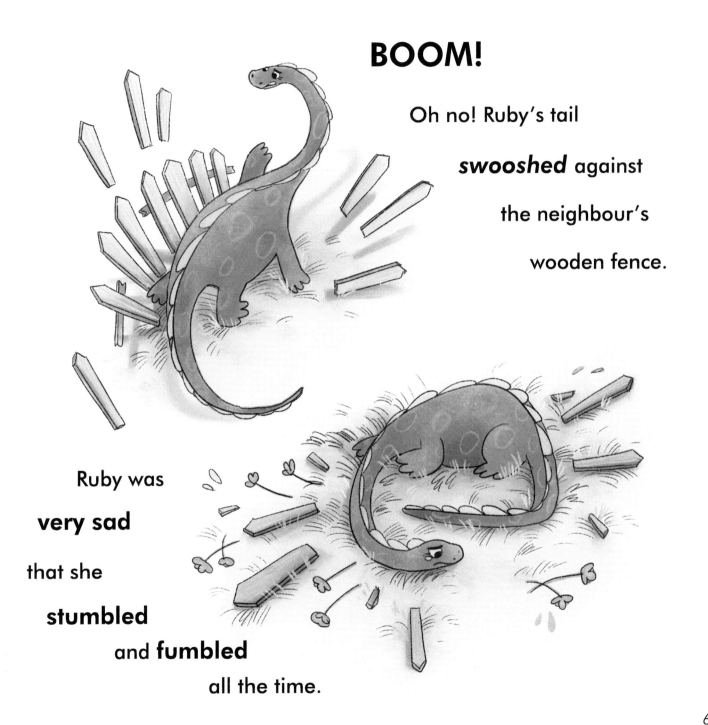

# BOOM!

Oh no! Ruby's tail *swooshed* against the neighbour's wooden fence.

Ruby was **very sad** that she **stumbled** and **fumbled** all the time.

But Archie had an idea. He approached his sad friend with something to cheer her up.

"Ruby, this spoon might not look very special on the outside, but what you can't see might surprise you."

Archie waved the spoon in the air.

**One, two, three...**
**...count with me...**

The spoon began to sparkle.

**Four, five, six...**
**...let's go quick...**

A bright light appeared.

**Seven, eight, nine...
...now is your time!**

10

Ruby's jaw dropped as she saw an extravagant valley filled
with sun-baked mountains, crispy grass, and juicy leaves!

She carefully watched her footsteps, worried that she might
break something. But Archie always stayed close by her side.

"Arrrgh!" yelled Archie, as he tripped over a pinkish-green blob.

Ruby rushed to help, but he just laughed and bounced back up to his feet.

"Look up!" said Archie.

Ruby's worries turned into wonder as she plucked some of their new discoveries from the trees.

"They taste sweeter than honey and totally delicious!" Archie said with his mouth full, "Let's call them...

## Raspberry-Pear Wapper-Zapper Crunchies!"

Slowly, Ruby grew **more** and **more** **curious** about what they would see and discover next.

For the first time, she was able to dance, spin and twirl in a large meadow.

She even helped Archie cross a wild river with her stretchy neck.

Then, they
bounced on jelly
wobbles and glided
on slippery ice lolly lakes.

In the distance, Ruby spotted a
mountain and followed the sweet
smell steaming from the top.

Archie huffed and Ruby puffed.
The journey up the mountain was tough.

Ruby nearly stumbled and Archie felt jumbled.
Oh! How they could hear their bellies grumble!

But they didn't give up and kept on going.
Till all of a sudden, it started snowing.

They realised that they had come too far to stop.
So they clawed their way to the very top.

Their reward was **better** than they could have ever imagined! Archie dipped his spoon into vanilla frosted apple crumble and Ruby munched on the juiciest apples.

Soon enough, their bellies were full.
And so was Ruby's heart.

At this moment, Ruby felt ready to go home.

One, two, three...
... count with me...
four, five, six...
... something is fixed...

21

seven, eight, nine...
...let your light shine!

22

Ruby felt different.
She wasn't scared.
And she wasn't sad
anymore.

Then, everyone helped to repair the backyard. Ruby danced with her stompy feet to make holes in the ground for Mum to plant new flowers.

After that, her long neck spun around to help Archie rebuild
the treehouse. Finally, Ruby twirled her strong tail to hold
up the new fence for Dad.

Feeling grateful, Archie and Ruby looked up at the stars and wondered where their next adventure would be.

Maybe on a rocket ship in outer space...
Or under the sea with rainbow fish and manta rays...

The possibilities were as endless as the night sky.

Archie and Ruby smiled.

26

"Archie..."

"Archie?"...

"Oh there's my wooden
spoon," said Mum.

"Shhh", said Dad, looking
over at Archie.

Dad gently carried him
up to his bedroom.

"Goodnight Archiesaurus,"
Dad whispered.

# For Parents/Teachers after reading:

Choose the activities below that match your child/student's reading needs:

Phonological awareness (Prepare my child/student's ability to hear, identify and manipulate individual sounds (phonemes) in words.

### Recommended for ages 3-5
Fundamental Phonological Awareness (Check my child/student's ability to hear, identify and manipulate the single letter individual sounds (phonemes) in words:

- Find as many "s" sound words as you can.
- Find as many "a" sound words as you can ("a" as in "apple" - short vowel sound).
- Find as many "t" sound words as you can.
- Find as many "p" sound words as you can.

### Recommended for ages 5-8
Advanced Phonological Awareness (Check my child/student's ability to hear, identify and manipulate individual sounds (phonemes) in words:

- Re-read page 17 to find all of the homophones and words that rhyme.
- Write a list of all of the words with the "or" sound including graphemes "or, au, our, aw"
- Write a list of all of the words with the "ch" sound including graphemes "ch, tch, ture"
- Write a list of all words with the long "e" sound including graphemes "ee, ea, ie, ey, y"

Ask your child/student to write a list of these words to help them to practise spelling and to reinforce their understanding of the sounds.

### Recommended for ages 5-8
Comprehension (Check my child/student's understanding of the text)

#### Literal questions:
- What does Archie do to cheer up Ruby? (Uses a wooden spoon to magically take them to a new world)
- How does Ruby help to repair the backyard? Give specific examples. (Her feet to make holes in the ground for flowers, her long neck to rebuild the treehouse and her strong tail to hold up the neighbour's fence)

#### Inferential questions:
- Where is the story set when Archie roars in the mirror? (Archie's bedroom)
- Why is Ruby upset on pages 5 and 6? (She keeps breaking things in the backyard)
- Why does Archie's dad call him Archiesaurus? (He loves dinosaurs and he goes on an adventure with his dinosaur friend)

### Recommended for all ages
Emotional Intelligence Questions:

- Using the card below, discuss what it means to be "emotionally resilient".
- Brainstorm different ways to show resilience and how you can show resilience every day (Example: trying a new sport or starting a conversation with a shy friend).
- How did Ruby learn resilience? (She developed a new inner confidence by trying new things with the support of her friend Archie and pushing through the challenges to get to the end reward).
- Write down a list of things that you already do, think or say or that you could change to build your resilience when you face new challenges.

**Su Pheng Lim**
*Author |* 🄾 *_sulimofficial*

**Christie Jia-Wen Tan**
*Illustrator |* 🄾 *christyyeee*

Su Pheng is an Australian Educator who enjoys using her spare time to write stories for children. She gets inspiration from her faith, travelling, and meeting people and kids from all cultures, backgrounds, and ages. She is passionate about the foundations of reading and giving kids the best start in life.

Website: http://www.sulim-uk.com/

Christie has a background in architecture and is currently based in London. She believes that every person or object has a story to tell and that architecture and many other creative expressions serve to tell those stories. Through her works, she seeks to invoke a sense of wonder in both children and adults. She has been an exhibiting artist in Malaysia, and is particularly known for her illustrations of the Buttermellow mice.

### What's next in the series?

Sign up on the website above to get more information about all of the upcoming adventures with Archie and his friends. The next book will focus on embracing diversity. Additionally, you and your kids can email Su directly about what your favourite part of Archiesaurus was and why.

## Collectible Cards

You can either cut it out or leave it in the book.

Value:
I am emotionally resilient

Story Meaning:
Ruby realises she has a problem with being too strong and breaking things, Archie goes with her on a challenging adventure where she learns that she can control her strength to repair what she had broken and build a better future.